Drive Me Crazy

and other short stories

Stefania Hartley

THE * SICILIAN * MAMA

ALSO AVAILABLE AS
EBOOK AND LARGE PRINT
BOOK

ISBN: 978-1-914606-24-3

These stories were first published individually in The People's Friend magazine.

Edited by Sandy Salisbury

Cover by Joseph Witchall

To my dad.

(1945-2022)

CONTENTS

1. PRESENT PREDICAMENT

Unlike most other Sicilians, Tanino and Melina had only one child. And the one daughter they had, had given them only one grandchild. No surprise that the little girl, Valentina, was the apple or, as they say in Italian, the pupil of their eye.

The only problem was that Tanino and Melina couldn't share even an apple, let alone an eye.

"What have you got Valentina for her birthday?" Tanino enquired with fake nonchalance, winding spaghetti around his fork.

Last year, Melina had told him that she had bought a Barbie doll. Later, he discovered that it wasn't any old Barbie doll: it came with an entire house, stables and horses.

"Some sewing stuff," Melina replied, also with fake nonchalance. She got up from the table, ostensibly to fetch the water jug, but more likely just to avoid his gaze.

Tanino remembered that Melina had given Valentina a sewing kit when she was four, so he guessed that the "sewing stuff" must be at least a sewing machine.

"Have you got her anything yet?" Melina asked.

"Not yet. Just thinking."

But Tanino had done much more than thinking: he had bought a new bicycle. He'd instructed the shopkeeper to keep the secret and had hidden the purchase at his brother's house.

It was a beautiful white bike with pink tassels, a pink basket and a detachable pink backrest. Even if Melina had bought an all-singing-and-dancing sewing machine, his bike was sure to come up trumps.

***

As she did every year on Valentina's birthday, Melina served a lavish lunch. A chocolate cake with sparkly candles finished the meal, but as far as Melina was concerned, the best was still to come: her birthday present.

Weeks before, her sister-in-law had informed Melina that a bicycle-shaped parcel had appeared in her house. Melina had immediately swapped the sewing machine she had bought for a bumper pack containing a sewing machine with attachments for embroidery and beadwork plus a circular knitting machine—all Barbie-branded. No bicycle could beat that!

Valentina was sitting politely on the sofa like a princess, waiting for the present-giving ceremony.

Melina scuttled into her bedroom and unearthed the enormous box. When Melina appeared on the threshold with the pink-wrapped parcel, Valentina jumped up and clapped her hands. "What is it, Nonna?"

"You'll have to find out." She watched her grandchild frantically tearing at the paper, grinning as she took in the contents of the box.

The little girl was speechless as she ran into her grandma's arms.

"You must teach her how to use it, Mamma, because I can't," Rosanna said.

"Of course I will," Melina replied, anticipating the pleasure of spending hours teaching Valentina all her sewing and knitting tricks.

"We haven't got space in our flat. Soon the people will have to move out to make room for the toys," Valentina's father commented dryly.

"No problem, we'll keep them here." Melina pointed to a table she had cleared for the purpose. Everything was going just as she'd hoped.

"I suppose I had better go and get my present now," Tanino said.

Valentina didn't hear him.

***

Tanino usually wished that his brother lived closer, but today he wished that it was further. He had no desire to return to his flat with the bike, only to have Valentina give it a cursory glance before returning to Melina's machines – not one, but two!

When he finally opened his door, Valentina rushed to him and tugged at his hand.

"We need your help because…" The little girl couldn't finish her sentence: she had seen the parcel and her eyes were sparkling. There was still a chance that his present wouldn't fare too badly against Melina's. "A bike! With a basket for my dolls!"

Valentina hopped on the saddle and started riding on the landing.

"Careful of the stairs!" Rosanna called.

Suddenly, one of the tassels caught in the tap of the floor's fire hose and was ripped off.

"It's broken!" Valentina's face crumpled.

"Don't worry, you can repair it with your

sewing machine," Tanino soothed.

At these words, Valentina burst into tears.

After he had left to collect the bike, Tanino learnt, problems had arisen with the sewing machine. Somehow the thread had got tangled in the bobbin and a spring had popped out of the rotating handle. All the adults had struggled to fix the machine, and Valentina had been left on the sofa alone. That was when Tanino had arrived with the bike.

"If I sew the tassel, will you fix the sewing machine?" Melina offered.

Of course," Tanino replied.

He fetched his toolbox and unscrewed the sewing machine's casing. Before Valentina's enthralled and apprehensive eyes, he inserted the spring back in and removed the knotted thread that had caused the accident.

Meanwhile, Melina pulled out her ancient sewing box and sewed the tassel back onto the bike.

***

That night, before falling asleep, Melina kissed Tanino. "You are an excellent grandfather."

"And you are an excellent grandmother. Valentina loves you to bits."

"She loves you, too."

"That's fine, then."

They smiled at each other and there was silence for a moment. Then Melina spoke.

"I have an idea," she said. "For her next birthday, shall we buy her something together?"

2. A LITTLE TEMPTATION

Tanino hadn't worn his suit trousers for ten years, and it showed. Buttoning them up without prolonged breath-holding was impossible.

Never mind. His wife would surely sort them out with needle and thread.

But Melina examined the garment, shaking her head. "I've already moved this button once. It can't go further."

"Maybe I can leave the button undone and hold the trousers up with a belt instead," Tanino suggested.

"The zipper might come open when you sit down."

That wasn't a risk he was willing to run in church at his nephew's wedding. "Then I'll buy a new suit," he announced.

Melina looked hard at him over her glasses. "Or you could lose some of that belly."

Losing some extra weight made sense, but

he didn't know where to start. Gym subscriptions and diet plans weren't for men in their seventies like him.

Losing a little weight surely didn't require rocket science. The trick was just eating less.

***

Melina had walked all the way to the furthest market in Palermo to buy panelle chickpea fritters from the best seller. She had bought them raw so that she could fry them at home and serve them to Tanino sizzling hot. He was going to love them.

But when Tanino saw them on the lunch table, his face fell.

He ate one fritter before claiming that he was full.

"Are you unwell?" Melina asked him.

"No. I'm very well."

It upset Melina when people didn't like her food. Perhaps he didn't trust purchased food as much as homecooked fare. She would cook Tanino's favourite pasta dish.

All afternoon, Melina pushed mint and garlic into the tuna with her fingers, then made a sauce of tomato and wine. That evening, when she served it, Tanino eyed his plate with apprehension.

"You've served me too much," he declared.

"Leave what you don't want," she replied,

trying not to sound piqued.

Tanino ate a couple of mouthfuls, then wiped his mouth on the napkin. "Thank you, dear."

"So little? If I had known you were going to eat like a sparrow, I wouldn't have filled your plate so much! It's going to go to waste!"

She stood up and whipped her napkin onto the table. "I know what the problem is: you've been eating at the café with your friends!"

"I haven't," he protested.

But Melina wasn't convinced. If Tanino was going to spoil his appetite at the café, she was going to cook even more mouth-watering delights than Carmelo, the café's owner.

***

Tanino stopped outside Carmelo's café and stared at the window. Now that he could no longer eat as much as he wanted, he noticed how many social occasions revolved around food. Meeting his friends at the café without ordering a pastry was impossible. He didn't have that kind of willpower.

Now that it was almost the Feast of All Souls, Carmelo's café overflowed with marzipan art. It was so lifelike that it looked like real strawberries, garlic bulbs and chestnuts. Unfortunately, though, they were still marzipan, so off-limits for him.

Tanino looked at the tempting window one last time, then walked away. He would not meet his friends at Lello's café until he could fit into his suit.

Now the mornings were unbearably long, especially as he could not spend them at home. If Melina was home, she would ask questions. If she wasn't, the tin of biscuits would talk to him instead.

So he spent the mornings strolling aimlessly down the town centre's pedestrian area, watching the bustling shops and trying not to look at the delis and cafés.

Even the street stalls were laden with sugar dolls and honey-glazed sweets at this time of year: all the gifts the ancestors would bring the children on the Feast of All Souls.

One morning, a display in a pharmacy's window caught his eye. Tins covered in pictures of ripe strawberries, curls of chocolate and vanilla pods were piled in a pyramid in the window. A cardboard cut-out of a beautiful lady promised:

No need to sweat, suffer and fast:
with our shakes, your weight loss will last!

In a flash, Tanino had a bag of Chocolate Chums, Strawberry Sensation and Vanilla Vibes shakes.

He made sure to return home when Melina

was out, and immediately tried Strawberry Sensation. It was delicious and filling. Now, if he didn't touch Melina's highly caloric food, he wouldn't starve.

***

"Are you sure you're alright?" Melina asked her husband when he walked past the plate of marzipan cherries and strawberries she had made for him.

"Just fine," he said, and sat on his chair without giving her marzipan creations a passing glance.

That night, in bed, Melina thought long and hard about how she could beat Carmelo.

It was almost morning when she had an idea. Carmelo would never buy out-of-season ingredients at a high price, as he wouldn't be able to recoup the cost.

The next day, she bought a large watermelon from South Africa, lugged it home and juiced it to make watermelon jelly. Tanino loved this Sicilian dessert for summer, and he would never find it at Carmelo's this time of year.

But that evening, Tanino took only one mouthful of the watermelon jelly, then declared himself full. Melina felt like screaming. Why wasn't her husband appreciating her cooking? Were her chocolate chips too old? Was her cinnamon powder stale?

The next day, Melina embarked on a kitchen pantry clear-out.

She pulled everything out of the kitchen cupboards, inspected expiry dates, and submitted everything to the sniff test.

At the very back of one of the cupboards, she came across some metal tins stripped of their labels. She opened them and sniffed them. They smelled delicious, but she couldn't remember what they were. In fact, she didn't even remember buying them. It wasn't safe to keep unlabelled foodstuff in the kitchen, so the tins ended up in the bin, too.

***

Tanino had his own secret mealtimes. He drank his shakes in the late morning, when Melina was out, so that he was full by lunchtime and could restrain himself.

She had been cooking increasingly delicious things, testing his resolve. It had taken superhuman effort to stop eating her watermelon jelly after just one spoonful. He had almost caved in and told her that he was on a diet, imploring her to refrain from cooking such mouth-watering dishes. But he had stopped himself just in time. What if she didn't take his diet seriously, or tried to dissuade him? He didn't want to risk it.

But as the novelty of the shakes was starting to wear off, he struggled more. The pleasure of food wasn't just in the taste and smell. Texture played a big part, too, and he was tired of having nothing solid to put between his teeth.

So when, one morning, he rummaged in the kitchen cupboard and found a bag of icing sugar and a jar of honey in the place of his slimming powders, he almost whooped. No more shakes!

But now he would have to think of a different way to lose the extra girth.

***

When Tanino was having his afternoon rest in front of the TV, an advert grabbed his attention.

A slimming suit promised results in two weeks. If losing weight could be as simple as wearing some plasticky long johns under his clothes, it was worth trying. He immediately rang the number and bought it.

A discreetly wrapped package arrived the next day. Tanino waited until Melina was out before unpacking it.

The wonder-suit smelled of plastic and crinkled. Nowhere in the TV ad had anyone mentioned that passers-by in the street would be able to hear it and smell it!

But the instructions sheet claimed that the

suit massaged your muscles, revived dead skin and created localised heat which melted the fat. Tanino was fired up with curiosity to find out if all that was true.

But after a day of wearing the squeaky, sticky suit, he concluded the "localised heat" wasn't melting the fat under his skin, but his whole person.

He decided to give the suit one more chance and wore it for another day. That evening, an extra-strength, anti-perspirant men's deodorant was left on his bedside table. He got the message and put the plastic suit where it belonged: the recycling bin.

***

Tanino stepped into his suit trousers and held his breath, not in anticipation, but in the attempt to keep his body inside them.

He had made progress: he could now button the trousers up. But the waist wasn't at all comfortable. He'd be mad to wear trousers that were tight before the wedding meal. Tanino sighed and resigned himself to buying a new suit.

Just then, Melina burst into the room. "Your brother is on the phone."

She still treated phone calls as the expensive and urgent affairs they used to be in the past. Tanino took the handset with the enthusiasm and speed of a sloth. Now he'd made the decision to buy a new suit, a dark cloud of gloom had enveloped him.

"Hello?"

"Hello, Tanino. You don't sound happy," Ciccio said.

"I can't fit into my suit, so I'll have to buy a new one for the wedding."

"Don't go anywhere. I'm on my way," his brother said, and ended the call before Tanino could say another word.

***

Not long after, Ciccio was at the door of their flat.

"This is the suit I was going to wear at Federico's wedding. It fitted me perfectly when I bought it two months ago. But with all the stress of the wedding preparations, I've lost weight and it's too baggy now. Perhaps it'll fit you." Ciccio extracted from the bag a beautiful smart suit.

Tanino tried it on and couldn't believe his luck when it fitted him perfectly. Ciccio also couldn't believe his luck when Tanino's suit fitted him perfectly and looked even better on him than the other one.

When Melina saw them, she scanned her husband and frowned. "Have you lost weight?"

"Not enough to fit into my old suit. God

knows I tried, though."

Melina raised her eyebrows. "You tried?"

"Yes, but let's not talk about it."

Melina clapped her hands together and grinned. "How did I not think about it? Silly me, I thought that you didn't like my cooking!" She rushed to the kitchen and immediately there came noises of pots and pans, as if she was about to cook up a storm.

"What's this all about?" Ciccio asked Tanino.

"I'm not sure, but I think you'd be wise to stay for dinner."

3. EVERY COCKROACH IS BEAUTIFUL TO ITS MUM

Melina was leafing through her favourite magazine when her gaze fell on an article and stayed there. The enlarged photo of a cockroach stared at her, sending shivers up and down her spine.

She hated cockroaches more than anything in the world. They rode up the sewage system and, bringing germs with them, entered people's homes and multiplied without permission. She hated their long feelers, always twitching and rotating, and she was positively frightened by their speed. She was convinced that she couldn't outrun one. The fact that they could also fly and possibly get tangled in her hair, was the stuff of her nightmares.

Finally, she couldn't bear the crunching noise they made when you squashed them with a slipper—not that she had ever done it: she wasn't brave enough to get that close.

How to prevent a cockroach infestation, the title of the article said. Melina read on voraciously. *Cockroaches are difficult to eliminate once they have started reproducing. If you see their babies, it's already too late.*

A chill rode up Melina's spine.

Cockroaches hate light and come out only in the darkness. You might have an infestation without realising it. To find out, surprise them by suddenly turning on the light in a dark room.

Melina scuttled to the bathroom, lowered the plastic roller blind until even the little holes in the slats were closed, and closed the door. She would return later for her ambush.

Cockroaches come out in summer so it's a good idea to cockroach-proof your home at this time of year and, in any case, always before the warm weather.

Where was this magazine printed? Rome. Oh, no! Palermo, where she lived, was warmer than Rome, and the hot weather had been here for some time! Could it be too late?

Tape the overflow holes of sinks and basins so that the vermin won't be able to come out. Plug every sink's plughole when not in use.

Melina rushed to plug every hole and vent in the flat, including the kitchen extractor.

If you have cockroaches, you can try this remedy: mix powdered match heads, flour and water and spread this cream on lettuce leaves, which cockroaches love. The phosphorus in the match heads will kill them…

Melina rushed to get matches, flour and water and worked meticulously on her potion, then lay the lettuce leaves in the dark corners of every room. But the article went on: *But if you have children or pets in your home, substitute this cream with a safer version made with chalk, sugar and water.*

Oh, no, they had a dog! Any moment now, her husband would be back from taking him for a walk. She must retrieve all the lettuce leaves!

In her panic she couldn't even remember where she had put them down.

***

"I'm ho-ome!" Tanino called from the door, with Bello padding in after him.

"Stay where you are!" his wife shouted from somewhere deep inside the flat. Her voice sounded muffled, which made Tanino desperately curious to find out what she was up to, so he did just the opposite of staying where he was.

"What are you doing with your head under the bed?"

"Ah!" She jolted in surprise and banged her head. "I told you to stay away!"

Melina slowly emerged with her hair messed up and a reddened face. In her right hand was a lettuce leaf covered in…was that ricotta?

"Are you on a diet?" he asked, unwisely.

"Are you suggesting that I should?" Her eyes were now speckled with fire.

"No, no. I just… don't understand what's going on."

Indecision marbled her face. She straightened her back, hauled herself up to sitting on her bed, and massaged her knees. "It's time for lunch," she said. Whatever she had been up to, she had decided not to tell him.

Had she lost something of his under the bed and was embarrassed to admit it? But what was the connection with lettuce and ricotta? Tanino went to wash his hands in the bathroom. Masking tape was stretched across the overflow hole. Aha. Melina's yearly fight against the roaches had begun.

***

The problem of how to deal with cockroaches in the home had always been a point of contention between them.

Tanino didn't appreciate cockroaches any more than his wife did, but he approached the issue with the fatalism that Sicilians are so famous for.

In his view, most problems had no solution and trying to find one was a waste of time and energies. His attitude was "live and let live".

The day the roaches stopped him enjoying his life, he would call the pest control people.

Unfortunately it wasn't the roaches that got in the way of his enjoyment of life, but his wife.

"You've left the sink unplugged! Remember the three B's: Bath, Basin, Bidet," she nagged every time he forgot to plug the sink after washing his hands.

With all the overflows taped, he was more concerned about forgetting to unplug the sink and flooding the bathroom.

One night, he was using the loo with the light off so as not to wake her, and was startled by her suddenly flicking the light on him, wielding a rolled magazine in her hands like a baton as if she was surprising a burglar.

"We don't have any cockroaches, Melina," he tried to reassure her.

"They're just waiting under the plugs for the moment we let the guard down."

Her obsession eventually rubbed on to him and, one night, he dreamed that he woke up to find himself transformed into a cockroach. He got very worried about such a wacky dream, until he remembered that he had read that same story in a book by some famous novelist—Kafka? —when he was a schoolboy.

***

"Help, Tanino!" his wife shrieked from the

bathroom.

Tanino shot out of his armchair, sending his crosswords and pen flying. Had she slipped in the bath? Got electrocuted? When he reached the bathroom door, he was prepared for the worst but not for what he found.

Melina had climbed inside the bidet's bowl and was staring petrified at three little cockroaches on the tiled floor.

"Kill them!" she urged.

She was like a distressed damsel up in the tower of a besieged castle, surrounded by attackers. Was Tanino meant to be her brave servant knight?

But he was unarmed and, even more importantly, he didn't feel at all brave. Cockroaches revolted him and he couldn't stand the sound they made when you squashed them. He would happily close the door and avoid using the bathroom until they had left.

But Melina demanded action.

Tanino went to the kitchen and reached into the cabinet under the sink for his trusted weapon: the insecticide spray. The canister would be his sword, while Melina's apron would be his shield.

"Quick, Tanino, quick!" she shrieked from the bathroom.

She was still perched on the bidet. "Darling,

get down or you're going to break the ceramic or, worse, fall off," he urged her.

"I can't, they're blocking my way," she whimpered.

Tanino shook his head and then the canister of insecticide.

"Wait! You're not going to use that, are you? I'm too close, and I have asthma."

Of course. He went back to the kitchen and swapped the insecticide with the broom—which, objectively, made a much better sword—then returned to rescue his damsel.

"Shoo, shoo," he said, pushing the little cockroaches towards a corner of the room.

"What are you doing?" she asked.

"Pushing them out of your way so you can get down from there."

"You mustn't just push them, you must kill them!" she roared. "They'll slip through the broom's bristles! Use your slipper, for heaven's sake!"

That was exactly what he didn't want to do. To squash them with his slipper, he would have to get closer to them than he was comfortable with, and he'd hear them crunch. But how could he admit that to anyone—even to his wife of fifty years—when men weren't supposed to be afraid of creepy crawlies. "It's too cruel, Melina. They're only babies."

"But disgusting ones."

"Not in their mother's eyes. Every cockroach is beautiful to his mum, the Neapolitan saying goes."

Melina's face mellowed. Then, as conflicting feelings churned inside her, it crumpled into an expression of utter desolation. Tanino couldn't bear seeing her in that state. He dropped his broom-sword and, overcoming his disgust for the insects, stepped into the bathroom.

The cockroaches scuttled away from his feet and hid behind the toilet.

"The coast is clear," he said, stretching his hand out to her.

She took it and climbed down from her tower.

"Where have they gone?" she asked.

"I'll deal with them once I've taken you away to safety," he said gallantly.

He accompanied her to the kitchen, sat her down and poured her a glass of water. When she had regained colour, he asked, "Will you be okay on your own if I leave you and deal with the creatures?"

She took his hand and whispered, "I admire you for being so goodhearted even to disgusting creatures. You don't have to kill them if you don't want to. You can just send them back to wherever it is they came from."

The look of admiration in her eyes was enough to melt Tanino's heart. There was no way he could use the insecticide spray now that Melina thought so highly of him. He marched back to the bathroom fervently hoping that the little beasties would be gone.

But they were still there. He took a deep breath, knelt to the floor and trapped each cockroach under an overturned glass.

Then Tanino placed the glass over the basin's plughole and, as soon as they had disappeared down it, he plugged it with lightning speed. One thing was certain: he would never forget to plug a sink again.

***

Melina thrust her magazine into her next-door neighbour's hand. "Take it. It tells you how to keep cockroaches out of your home."

"Thank you, Melina. But don't you need it?" Giovanna asked.

"No. I have Tanino. He's the 'cockroach whisperer'."

"Lucky you!"

Later that day, the doorbell rang. It was Giovanna.

"Melina, guess what? I've just found an entire family of cockroaches in my bathroom. Oh, how I wish I had plugged the holes! Can I borrow Tanino to get rid of them, please?"

"Of course," Melina answered, full of pride. Clearly not all husbands were as brave and capable as hers.

"Tanino, your help is required next door," she announced, bursting into the sitting room where he was relaxing with his crosswords.

"What for?" he asked, scrunching his forehead in puzzlement.

"Giovanna has found a whole family of cockroaches in her bathroom. I told her that you are wonderful with cockroaches—I knew you would be happy to help."

It was probably just a trick of the light, but Tanino's face suddenly looked very pale.

4. GET ME TO THE CHURCH ON TIME

Melina wondered whether the death of "till death us do part" had to be of natural causes. Today, her husband was pushing her into "murderous thoughts" territory.

"We're going to be late to the christening!" she shouted through the door of the bathroom where he had barricaded himself.

"It's okay. It won't start without us," he said.

"That is the problem!" The ceremony wasn't going to start without the godparents. No chance of sneaking in late at the back of the church, undetected. They would be holding up all the guests, the baby's parents, the priest and—heaven forbid—the baby!

Being late would be a major embarrassment and, if there was anything Melina dreaded more than war, plagues and the dentist, it was embarrassment.

"My patience is wearing thin, Tanino," she warned her husband. Today her patience and good mood had already been thinned by the hot Scirocco wind blowing to Sicily from Africa. Despite being early June, it was too hot for wearing tights and closed shoes. But bare legs and sandals wouldn't do for the occasion. She had bought the coolest tights she could find—10 denier—and had bravely put them on, but she was already suffering.

The landline rang. It felt like an alarm warning them that they were running late. She didn't pick up. Even if she had had time to chat, she wasn't in the mood.

The toilet flushed and, a little later, Tanino emerged, smiling. "What are we waiting for? Let's go" he said.

***

The christening was in a village a few kilometres outside Palermo. Tanino took the motorway exit without hesitation.

"Are you sure you know the way?" Melina asked.

"Absolutely. I spent a whole summer in that village as a lad."

"Who did you stay with?"

"My friend, Girolamo. We met doing national service. Sadly, we lost touch."

As they travelled, the road signs and markings faded, and the road surface became warped by the heat of many summers.

"What did that orange sign say?" Melina asked.

Tanino hadn't read it. "Probably nothing important."

The provincial road wound up and down a hill.

"Stop!" Melina shouted as they went round a bend.

A herd of goats was crossing the road. Tanino slowed down a little, calculating that the animals would be gone before he got to them.

But they weren't gone. He came to a stop. The goatherd seemed to be struggling to keep control of the animals who, instead of going across the road, had decided to escape down it.

"I must help the man," Tanino cried.

***

Melina watched in disbelief as Tanino, with his arms stretched wide, corralled the goats back towards the goatherd. She should be sitting in the church listening to the happy peal of the belfry, not sitting in the car listening to the clanging of some rebel goats' bells.

She wound down the window and a gust of hot wind ruffled her hair. So much for her early morning hairdresser appointment! She closed the window, enduring the heat instead.

Once the goats were all safely across to the

other side of the road, Tanino emerged from the scrubby road verge, dusting his trousers. Oh, no. Now they would look scruffy, too.

Tanino walked to Melina's side of the car. "I'm sorry, but we have to walk the last bit. The road ahead is closed. The goatherd told me. It must be what the orange sign was about. The village is just the other side of these fields. We'll be there soon," he reassured her.

Reluctantly, Melina took his hand and uncurled herself out of the car.

"The road is closed to pedestrians, too. We've got to go through the fields."

***

Melina's blood was boiling, and not just because of the heat.

Her heeled shoes were not made for the dusty, cracked soil of the Sicilian countryside, and her silk dress wasn't made for brushing against thistles.

Then came the barbed wire. Tanino pressed it down with his foot, but one of the barbs caught on her tights and pulled a hole. She had to bite her tongue not to say improper words.

Next came the agave plants. Brushing past their spiky leaves, Melina got a second hole in her tights.

The third hole was made by the prickly pear cactuses that grew like a wall. Tanino pushed some of the prickly stems out of her way with a stick, but there were just too many. This third hole was on the top of her knee, so it was going to become enormous as soon as she bent her knee in church.

When they finally emerged from the scrub, Tanino's trousers were furry with sticky seeds, his slicked-down hair had been lifted by the wind, and his forehead was beaded with sweat. Melina could only imagine how she looked.

"We can't show up at the church in this state."

Tanino scanned her. "You look lovely."

They must have stopped too close to a nest, because two birds screeched angrily above their heads. A moment later, something splattered on Melina's shoulder!

"This is the best I can do without water. I'll take the rest off when we get to the church," Tanino said, his handkerchief now soiled.

"But the people waiting outside the church will see me arrive in this state."

"Well, I remember the house where Girolamo's parents lived. If the family still live there, they might let us use their bathroom," Tanino suggested.

If Tanino's friend or his family still lived in the house, they couldn't just use the toilet and dash off. There were going to be hugs, kisses, and reminiscences, which would make them ever later. No, it wouldn't do. They couldn't start their godparenting job arriving late for the christening.

She would have to turn up at the church as she was—with windswept hair, holes in her tights, and a soiled right shoulder. "No, let's go as we are."

***

"Have they started without us?" Tanino wondered aloud.

The church doors were closed and nobody was outside.

"They can't start without the godparents. Are you sure that this is the right place?" Melina asked.

"Absolutely."

They tried the doors but they were locked, so they knocked at the presbytery.

The priest opened the door with a napkin round his neck.

"We were told there would be a christening in this church," Tanino said.

"Oh, yes!" The priest smiled. "But you're early. Because of the road closure, the christening has been postponed to this afternoon. Has nobody informed you?"

"The phone rang just as we were leaving…but I didn't answer," Melina admitted sheepishly.

Tanino checked his mobile phone. He had forgotten to turn it on.

Just then, a man came up behind the priest. He stopped and stared at Tanino.

"Is it Tanino?" the man asked tentatively.

"Girolamo!"

They hugged, kissed and patted each other's backs.

"What are you doing here?" Girolamo asked.

Tanino told him about the christening.

"I'm the sacristan here. I've just finished preparing the church for the christening," Girolamo said. "Come and have lunch with my sister and me, then we'll walk back together," he offered.

"Thank you," Tanino said enthusiastically. "And you won't mind us using your bathroom to freshen up?"

***

Melina would have never agreed to be introduced to one of Tanino's friends and his sister in her current state. Would there be any end to her embarrassment?

All the way to Girolamo's house, the two men reminisced about their national service while Melina thought of ways she could make herself more presentable.

She took off her jacket and folded it inside out so that the stain was hidden. She tried to pull her tights up to hide some of the holes, but it was impossible while walking. She resigned herself to staying as she was.

Carla remembered Tanino and was extremely excited to meet Melina.

After whipping up a delicious lunch, she found a new pair of tights for Melina—only seven denier!—and a soapy cloth to clean her dress. Melina started to have faith that she might not embarrass herself at the christening after all.

"Could I borrow a hairbrush?" she asked.

The other woman's face lit up. "Yes, but I have a better idea: a hat!"

Melina hated hats, but Carla had already gone off to fetch it. This hat was big, red and frilly. It reminded Melina of a poisonous red mushroom and it certainly didn't go with her purple dress. But Carla put it on Melina's head and smiled. "Perfect!"

Then she rushed out into the garden and returned with a red hibiscus flower, which she pinned to Melina's jacket. It was big, bright and attention-grabbing: everything she didn't want. But could she refuse it without compromising a budding friendship?

"Thank you," Melina said.

"Don't you look great?" Carla asked her.

Melina looked at herself in the mirror. She no longer looked like she had been dragged through the bushes, but now she looked like a doll dressed by a child. "Er… yes."

Carla called Tanino over. "What do you think?"

"She looks lovely," Tanino said, causing Carla to grin, little knowing that Tanino had said the same thing when Melina had just emerged from the fields.

Melina thanked Carla, and set off with Tanino and Girolamo.

Tanino squeezed her hand. "You're lovely, as always," he said tenderly.

Melina's heart swelled a little. She might not be well dressed, but she was loved, and that was all that mattered.

***

Going to the church with Girolano meant that they arrived before anyone else.

"We're not late after all," Tanino commented smugly.

When the ceremony started, baby Annabella began to grizzle. Her mum and dad passed her to each other, but it didn't help. To their amazement, it was only when they passed her to Melina that Annabella stopped crying.

From then on, the ceremony went smoothly

while Annabella stared, enthralled, at the frilly brim of Melina's hat and the bright red hibiscus on her jacket.

5. SHIFTING SANDS

It was the 7th of August, feast day of St. Cajetan, the saint after whom Tanino was named.

He was planning to spend his special day sitting on his balcony, under the shade of his new awning, admiring his geranium and lavender pots and answering phone calls wishing him a happy Saint's Day.

He couldn't understand why, as soon as the hot August days arrived, everyone left the Sicilian capital for the beach. Why not install an awning on their balconies and enjoy the breeze from the comfort of their own flats? No long drives, no pesky sand, no crowds.

He was just opening his deckchair when Melina popped her head out of the French doors.

"Don't sit down, dear. Get into your swimmers and pack a towel. We're going on a trip," she said with a grin.

“Pardon?” Tanino hadn’t worn his swimmers since their forty-five-year-old daughter was a child.

“Giovanna and Luigi have invited us to spend the day at their beach hut to celebrate your Saint’s Day.”

Tanino hated the seaside—all that salt, sun and crowds!

Sand sneaked into every crack of your body and, with sun lotion and sweat, it turned you into a breaded cutlet.

Unfortunately, Melina loved the beach. Tanino had often wondered why nobody had thought of including the question “do you like the mountain or the sea?” in marriage preparation courses.

“It’s kind of Giovanna and Luigi to invite us, but I’m very happy at home.”

“You need some sunshine, dear. It gives you Vitamin D.”

“And skin cancer.”

She huffed. “It’s not good for you to stay indoors all the time.”

“I’m not indoors. I’m on the balcony, which is suspended in the air.”

“Giovanna and Luigi are waiting for us downstairs and”—Melina smiled, knowing she had him—"I’ve made a pasta bake for our lunch.”

There was no way he would miss out on his wife's pasta bake, so he trudged to the bedroom and got into his swimmers.

***

Why did Tanino have to be so grumpy when Melina had organised this wonderful outing? She had never met anyone so resistant to swapping their slippers for swimming flippers. Why was her husband attached to his flat like a limpet?

"Why all this traffic?" he grumbled, as they queued on the road that led out of Palermo city to Mondello Beach.

"Everyone is going to the beach. It's the place to be when it's hot." She clacked her hand fan open with a sharp movement and started fanning herself.

"Collective madness."

"A little traffic is a small price to pay."

"Easy for you to say—you're not the one driving."

"We can swap," Melina volunteered, knowing that neither of them liked it when she was at the wheel.

"Another time."

The traffic light turned red just before they reached it and Tanino sighed. If he continued being grumpy when they got to the beach, Melina would leave him with Luigi and spend time with Giovanna.

She wasn't going to let her grumbling husband ruin the outing for her.

***

By the time they'd fought their way through the traffic, found parking and met Giovanna and Luigi, Tanino was drenched in sweat. He stepped cautiously on the raised walkway leading to the rented huts: those wooden planks were the only barrier between him and the hot sand below. Unfortunately, the walkway stopped well before Giovanna and Luigi's hut. Walking on the sand was a battle.

"How far do we have to go?" Tanino complained.

"Walking on sand strengthens your calves," Melina replied.

His calves were already burning, and not just from the sunshine. "Isn't sand made of tiny broken shells?"

"I think so."

"And isn't glass made with molten sand?"

"So I've heard."

"So we're walking on broken glass," Tanino concluded.

Melina shot him a glare.

"Here we are!" Luigi announced, pointing to a row of identical beach huts. How could he be sure which was his?

"Let's leave our stuff here and go for a swim," Giovanna suggested.

"Tanino can't swim," Melina announced.

"Nonsense!" Tanino protested, feeling his cheeks heat up.

In his list of pet hates, the sea came a close second after sand. It was a treacherous mass of brine which left you shivering, sticky and sore when you got out. But if Luigi, Giovanna and Melina were going to swim, he would jolly well swim too.

"Of course I can swim! I just haven't done a lot of it lately."

The last time he swam was when he was a boy, but there was no reason he couldn't still do it.

They pulled out deckchairs, put bags and clothes in the hut and set off to the water's edge.

Stepping barefoot on the sand was like walking on hot coals. Tanino hopped quickly from one foot to the other, and when he plunged his feet into the sea, he thought that he could hear the hissing sound of steam.

"Walking on the sand rubs the dead skin off the soles of your feet. It's a free pedicure," Melina said.

"It felt like it was rubbing more than the dead skin off my feet," he said wryly.

"You're being a wet blanket. I'm going to join the others," she snapped.

A wet blanket to wrap himself in was just what Tanino wished for.

He watched the other three swim to the pontoon. All that effort, and for what? Salt in their eyes and shivers through their bodies.

He had never understood what the point of the salt in the sea was. All those nosy little fish swimming around his legs surely could find better things to do than harassing bathers! He took a step away from them. Someone ought to teach them about personal space and privacy. Well, at least they weren't jellyfish. Oh dear—what if there were jellyfish in the water? He hadn't heard anyone raise the alarm, but someone always had to be the first…

A beach ball bounced on the water and landed in front of him.

"Ball, please!" People were shouting from the beach, waving at him. The ball was floating within arm's reach.

Tanino stretched a hand to grab it, but the ball rolled away. He needed to get a firm grip with both hands. As he stepped towards it, the water pushed the ball away again.

Conscious of the people watching from the beach, Tanino grew frantic, which only made the situation worse. In the end, he caught the ball by pouncing on it and getting a faceful of seawater.

"Got it!" he called out triumphantly. But where had the people gone? Chasing the ball, he had moved along the shore and didn't recognise the beach anymore. Someone ran towards him and Tanino finally returned the ball.

By now he was soaked, his eyes were stinging and he had had enough of the water. Melina and the others were so far out that he decided to go back to their beach hut and sit on a deckchair.

But where was it? From the sea, everything on the beach looked the same.

He waded back to the shore and trudged up and down the water's edge. Now he remembered why he hated the sea almost as much as the sand: it made the sand stick to your body.

Eventually, he found their beach hut. How strange: he was sure that they had put out four deckchairs, not two. Tricks of the memory!

He sat down, lay back and closed his eyes against the sun's glare. A little later, he heard a voice saying hello.

Tanino opened his eyes. A stranger stood before him with a tray wrapped in the bakery's paper. Judging by the smell, it contained mini pizzas and sausage rolls. Was it normal at the beach to be greeted by strangers? He didn't have a clue about beach etiquette.

"Hello."

"Are you a friend of Luigi?"

"Yes. I'm Tanino. Nice to meet you."

The man shook his hand. "Salvatore. So it's your Saint's Day today."

"Yes."

"Have a mini pizza."

"Oh, that's very kind. Thank you." Things were finally looking up for him.

***

Melina was starting to get worried. Tanino wasn't in the sea and he wasn't at their beach hut either.

"He must be lost," Giovanna said. "It's easy to do. I told the management company that we ought to be allowed to personalise our beach huts, but they won't have it."

"Let's split up and search for him. If we can't find him on the beach, we'll start looking in the water," Luigi suggested.

In the water! Melina's head spun with dread as she imagined the worst. She shouldn't have trusted Tanino when he said that he could swim. She shouldn't have let him out of her sight.

All her irritation at her husband's

grumpiness instantly fizzled away. She closed her eyes and prayed to St Cajetan. "Surely you wouldn't like another saint with the same name, so please let me find Tanino alive."

***

His wife's pasta bake was on another level, but she still wasn't back and Tanino was hungry so he was enjoying the baker's pizzas and Salvatore's company.

"Luigi is back," Salvatore said.

Tanino turned to the sea, where a man dripping from a swim was walking towards them. But he wasn't Luigi.

"Luigi, I've just met your friend, Tanino," Salvatore said.

Tanino and the man looked at each other, equally puzzled.

"Do we know each other?" the man asked Tanino.

A terrible suspicion crept into Tanino's mind—and a quick glance through the beach hut's open door confirmed it. This wasn't Luigi and Giovanna's hut.

Tanino felt his cheeks on fire. "I am terribly sorry; there's been a mistake."

Just then, Melina's voice pierced the air. "Tanino! What are you doing?"

She looked wild: mussed hair, flushed cheeks, red eyes. Tanino wondered if she looked like that because she had spent too long in the sea, because she was worried about him or because she had caught him eating other people's mini pizzas instead of her pasta bake.

Tanino dropped the remains of the pizza.

***

Melina invited the two strangers to lunch with them, but they politely refused. Tanino thanked the men and followed her to Luigi and Giovanna's hut.

"I thought you had drowned, my darling." Melina brushed the sand off his chest as if it were the dust from a battle. "Tell me: can you swim?"

"In all truth, I don't know."

"I'm sorry I've dragged you here on your Saint's Day when you don't like the sea. We could leave if you like."

"Not before we eat your pasta bake," he said.

Melina smiled, pleased that he hadn't forgotten about her pasta. "Yes, but we can leave after lunch if you want."

"Actually, I'd like to find out if I can still swim first."

"Good idea."

***

After a siesta under the beach umbrella to digest Melina's delicious pasta bake, Tanino ventured into the water. This time, Melina was right behind him.

"Keep the fish distracted, Melina."

She stomped and splashed. Whether it deterred the fish, Tanino had no idea, but it was impossible for him to see the creatures, which was just as good.

When the water level reached his neck, Tanino lifted his legs and started kicking. He floated!

"I can do it!"

"You can do it!"

Every now and then, he touched the sandy seafloor with the tip of his big toe, just to make sure that it was still there. The pontoon didn't look at all far now.

"Shall we swim to the pontoon, Melina?"

"You don't want to go home?"

"It would be a pity to leave so soon. I want to enjoy my Saint's Day, after all."

6. DRIVE ME CRAZY

"Tanino, do you know that Giovanna got a ruby from Luigi for their ruby anniversary?" Melina said when she got back from church.

Oh, no. The 29th of this month would mark their 55th wedding anniversary.

Tanino wondered what expensive stone a 55th wedding anniversary would be named after, but he didn't need to ask—Melina volunteered the information.

"Fifty-five years is an emerald anniversary. Emerald symbolises eternity and commitment."

Was that because sticking together for fifty-five years felt like an eternity? Tanino thought better of saying this.

It wasn't that he didn't love Melina. On the contrary, he would give not one but both his kidneys for her, and lungs, too (the heart, he had already given her).

But he didn't believe in soppy romanticism.

For him, love was cooking the other person's favourite meal—the Sicilian pasta with sardines and fennel was his. Changing the lightbulb of her bedside lamp so that she could read in bed. Helping look for a misplaced pair of reading glasses.

"Who decided on emeralds? The jewellers?" he grumbled.

"You're not funny."

"I'm not joking. It was a diamond mining company that started the fashion of diamond engagement rings, did you know?"

"Well, the next big anniversary after emerald is diamond." Melina thrust a magazine under his gaze. On a page, all the wedding anniversaries were laid out on a table and matched with a mishmash of materials that ranged from cotton to platinum.

Tanino shook his head. "It makes no sense: when a man is young and still in employment, the anniversaries are cheap stuff like cotton, paper and leather. But when the poor fellow is retired, he has to dish out rubies, emeralds and diamonds. If you ask me, this is all completely topsy-turvy."

"It's not. The longer the people have been together, the bigger the prize," Melina said smugly.

"Because marriage is an endurance race, of

course," he teased.

She snorted and strode off to the kitchen.

Tanino trudged to the balcony to tend his roses, wondering if there would be any dinner for him that night.

***

Why couldn't Tanino be a little more romantic? Men were such cheats: they gave you flowers, sang love songs and murmured sweet nonsense into your ears when they were courting you, only to stop once they'd secured you in marriage.

They turned from Cupid, the Roman god of love, to Mars, the god of war—that was when, heaven forbid, they didn't turn into Bacchus, the god of wine!

Melina let out a sigh and her nostrils filled with a smell of burning. Oh, no, she had burned the dinner!

Oh, well, Tanino didn't like lentils anyway, and she didn't mind if they were a little 'roasted'. Tanino would complain, though. He had become very fussy about food. Her mamma had warned her: as they grow old, men think of nothing but what they're having for their next meal.

Melina shook off her reverie and drained the pasta, which had irreparably turned to gloop.

***

When Tanino sank his fork into the white and brown goo he could hardly tell that it was pasta with lentils. His least favourite food, and now it was cooked to death, too.

But he refrained from any comment. This was clearly his punishment for teasing Melina about wedding anniversary gifts.

"What happened to the mandolin that you used to serenade me with when you were young? Have you still got it?"

Tanino frowned. Where was this conversation going? "No. Our daughter rode her tricycle over it."

"Ah, yes." Melina's face lit up. "We should buy you another one."

"Wouldn't the money be better spent on a new shopping trolley? One of the wheels looked wobbly when you came back from the market yesterday."

"The wheel is the least of its problems: the handle came off while I was crossing the road."

Tanino's heart squeezed as he imagined Melina struggling with a runaway trolley in the midst of zooming cars.

"But I've repaired it," she added, lifting her chin.

This was even more worrying. The last time Melina had 'repaired' something, she had used sticky tape and jute string on a kitchen pot's handle.

"Pity about the mandolin," she said with a slightly theatrical sigh.

Tanino felt defensive. Was she accusing him of deliberately not replacing the broken mandolin?

"It's lucky at least that I have dried and kept the flowers you gave me on our first date." She tutted.

Tanino felt at a loss about Melina's logic. What was the connection between the broken mandolin and the dried flowers? Were they talking about the durability of objects? About preserving stuff from the past? "There are some nice things from my mother's flat in the garage, if you want to take a look."

Melina shot him a narrowed-eyed look.

"There's none more deaf than the one who doesn't want to hear," she hissed, then got up to clear the table.

Tanino, puzzled but relieved that that the meal was over, got up and went to the store cupboard to check on Melina's trolley.

***

Melina didn't sleep well. How could Tanino be so insensitive?

He didn't care about her anymore. He only cared about his plants, which he watered and checked every night for parasites. He collected rain just to water them, and squashed any aphids he found between his forefinger and thumb with infinite patience.

The next morning, Melina picked up her shopping list and her handbag, then went to the store cupboard to get her trolley.

The wool that she had used to tie the handle had disappeared. Melina gave it a little tug and found that the handle didn't come off. Tanino must have done something to it. Was he trying to say that her repair wasn't good enough?

At the market, Pippo the fishmonger saw her coming. "Signora Melina, my swordfish is so fresh that the sardines in its stomach are still swimming!" he sang to her in his operatic baritone.

"Then I shall have the sardines, because they'll cost me less," she answered.

It was part of their normal banter preceding a sale. In the end, she would usually buy what he recommended, but only after making him shave something off the price.

"Swordfish is your husband's favourite," he retorted.

"Today isn't his birthday. He can eat sardines."

But Pippo had cut two generous slices of swordfish and wrapped them in waterproof paper. "I'll give you a good price, my lady. How much do you want to pay for these?"

"Five euros."

"Eight."

"Seven."

"Seven fifty."

A beat of silence and the price was agreed.

Just as Melina opened her wallet to pay, a hand landed on her shoulder.

"Melina, my dear, how are you?"

It was Giovanna. Immediately, Melina's eyes swivelled to her friend's left hand, where an eternity ring studded with rubies and diamonds winked coquettishly at her. Melina felt a cold and spiky lump of envy, hard and green as an emerald, embed in her chest.

"Your swordfish is ready, my beautiful lady," Pippo's gravelly voice boomed.

He had called her 'beautiful'. When was the last time Tanino had paid her any compliment?

The fishmonger smiled jovially, Giovanna's ring twinkled in the sunlight, and Melina's resentment boiled like ruby-red hot lava.

"I've changed my mind. I want sardines," she said.

Pippo rolled his eyes and, holding a hand to his chest, groaned as if he had been hit in the heart by an arrow. "My heart aches, but your wish is my command."

Back home, the fennel fronds endured a

vicious chopping, the soaked sultana were squeezed almost dry in Melina's fists, and the sardines' backbones were shot into the bin like arrows as Melina took out on them her frustration against her wicked husband.

***

Tanino found himself standing in front of the jeweller's window without knowing how or why he had got there.

He had left the house to buy a new plant for the balcony but found himself walking past the jeweller's. The window glittered and twinkled like a galaxy. It was a sight to behold but, as in every galaxy, there were black holes—the plastic tags with the prices: 599 euros, 1,999 euros.

The only things that were remotely affordable were simple chains and plain silver or gold bands. Well, there was no way he was going to spend hundreds of euros on a green stone and some yellow metal. He swivelled on his heels and walked on to the plant shop where he bought a luxuriant potted rose, then went back home.

When the lift doors opened on to his floor the unmistakable scent of sardines and wild fennel filled his lungs.

Could he be so lucky that the smell was coming from his flat? There were two apartments on his floor and the chances that Melina would be cooking his favourite dish today, of all days, were near zero.

Yet when he opened the door of his flat, the smell of wild fennel and fish meandered through the red rose plant in his arms and dived straight into his nostrils.

"I'm ho-ome!" he called from door.

This was the signal for Melina to drop the pasta in the boiling water. She would only do it when he got home because, once the pasta was in, dinner could not be delayed.

Without changing into his slippers or even putting the heavy plant down, he scuttled into the kitchen. There was his Melina, bent over the bubbling pot, energetically stirring the pasta. For him.

Tanino's heart filled with song. "My darling, oh, how I love you when you cook for me!" he cried.

Melina whipped her head round. As her surprised gaze slipped from his face to the roses he was holding, a smile curled her lips and her eyes lit up.

With rare quickness of thought he thrust the blooming pot towards her. "For you!"

Melina dropped her wooden spoon and her smile reached the wrinkles on the sides of her eyes. "Oh, Tanino! You shouldn't have!" she said, taking the plant from him.

Then he hugged her and kissed her like he hadn't done in a while.

***

On their anniversary Melina felt contented. Looking at it from a practical angle, a plant was better than a bunch of flowers because it would continue to flower year after year—especially if it came with the warranty that Tanino would be looking after it lovingly for her.

As they sat at the table eating *pasta con le sarde* again and drinking wine, she admired her rose on the balcony. It now had more flowers than on the day she had received it. Then, she had a jolt.

"Tanino, I've only just noticed! The flowers are red like rubies, and the leaves are green like emeralds. Oh, aren't you a hopeless romantic!"

7. A COUNTRY RETREAT

"If I wasn't desperate, I wouldn't ask you, Melina," Giovanna told her with a shake of her head which made her earrings tinkle, "because I know how busy you are, but you and your husband are the only ones left in this building in August. If you could water my plants, I would really appreciate it."

Melina had already agreed to water the plants of another neighbour, collect the mail of the flat below and drop in to check on the flat above, which sometimes had water leakages.

All this was because she and Tanino didn't leave their flat, even in August, when the city emptied.

"If the sun is too strong on the sitting room balcony, can you move the roses to the kitchen balcony?" her neighbour went on. "And don't forget to add a drop of fertiliser in the water once a week. If the scirocco wind comes, push the pots closer to the wall, otherwise the wind will tip them over and you'll have to scoop all the soil back in, which has happened to me a few times. Thank you so much, Melina."

Giovanna thrust a bunch of keys into Melina's hand before Melina had even agreed. "Melina, I feel like crying. I've got so much to do: covering all the furniture with dustsheets, putting mothballs in cupboards, emptying the fridge… A second home is such a lot of work!" Giovanna sighed dramatically. "Sometimes I even envy you."

Even? Melina felt a little offended.

"I'd better get on with it. Thank you for your help, Melina!" Giovanna patted Melina's arm and disappeared into her flat.

Melina grumbled under her breath, stuffed Giovanna's keys in her bag and went on her way.

Meeting Giovanna had made Melina late for church, which only added to her irritation. She was about to take her usual place in her usual pew when Elena intercepted her.

"Melina, just the one I was looking for!"

"What's the matter?" Melina answered stiffly, expecting to be asked to read, collect the offertory money or do some other task for the parish.

"In August, Father Pietro is going to his sister's in the mountains and we need someone to open the church for the priests who will cover for him."

"Have you asked Peppina?" Melina replied grumpily.

"She's going to her villino by the sea."

"Rosaria?"

"She's going to her cottage in the country. All the others will be away, too, and I'm going to my brother on the southern coast. You are the only one left in Palermo."

If Elena had told her she'd be shipwrecked on a deserted island like Robinson Crusoe and have to live there for 28 years, Melina would have felt less alone. But she wasn't the kind of woman who moaned and whined when she was unhappy.

"What makes you think that I might not be away?" she retorted defiantly.

"You hate travelling and you don't own a holiday home."

"You make lots of assumptions about me," Melina replied.

The idea of jumping on a train and booking herself and Tanino into a B&B was forming in her mind, even if it terrified her.

"Is there something you haven't told me?" Elena narrowed her eyes, smiling.

Melina raised an eyebrow. "Perhaps. I can't say anything at this stage."

Her friend smiled. "I see," she said, tapping her nose as the bell of the Mass rang.

As Father Pietro walked to the altar, Melina prayed. "Please, God, give me a little place in the country where Tanino and I can spend the month of August."

Later, after the part of the Mass in which everyone thinks about their sins, she changed her petition. "Please, God, don't do it for me, but for Tanino. He'd love a little garden of his own, and he deserves it. Do it for our granddaughter—she'd love to have somewhere to ride her bike and she's worked hard at school."

After Mass, on the way home, Melina stopped by the bakery for the evening bread.

"Signora Melina, please be aware that I'll be closed for two weeks starting this coming Monday," the baker told her. "We're going to our villino by the sea which we share with my brother and his family."

For the first time in her life, the smell of freshly baked bread made Melina feel sick and, by the time she got home, she was in a temper.

"You could at least have laid the table for supper," she told Tanino, who was watching a property programme.

"I never lay the table," he said, confused.

"All the worse for that!"

***

Tanino ran a hand over his face and braced himself for a difficult suppertime. What could he have done wrong this time? It wasn't Melina's birthday or their anniversary, that much he knew, so what could he have missed? "Are you upset about something? I mean, other than the unlaid table."

"Do you think that the unlaid table is not enough to be upset about?"

"No."

"Well, I'm also upset because everyone is going away to their summer houses and we're left here to look after their plants, their post and to open the church for the visiting priest. The only people left in this roasting hot city in August will be the burglars, the inmates and us."

"No need to open the church, then," he joked, but she didn't smile. "I'm sorry, dear. You should have married a doctor or a solicitor if you were so keen on owning a villino."

"That's not true: the baker has one," Melina retorted.

"It's the farm where he was born. He was moaning to me the other day that he and his brother spend their holidays repairing it, working like slaves."

"Peppina and Rocco have a villino too, and

he's a greengrocer."

Tanino shook his head. "It's just an allotment where he grows some of his fruit and vegetables."

"But they have a house there."

"A glorified garden shed."

"I'd be happy with that." Melina crossed her arms.

Tanino got up from his chair and wrapped an arm around Melina's shoulders. "I have a friend who has a house in the mountains. It was his parents' home and, from what I understand, it's empty. I can ask him if he would like to let it to us for a couple of weeks."

Melina's frown stretched into a smile. "Yes, please!"

Tanino smiled too, even though he knew this wasn't the happy ending yet. If Melina enjoyed her stay, she'd ask to return. And if she enjoyed it very much, she would pine for a place of their own.

***

"Melina!"

"Peppina! How are you? Are you calling me from your villino?" Melina asked down the phone.

"I'm very disappointed in you, Melina. I never would have imagined that you'd do this to me."

"Do what?"

"Make me find out from other people instead of telling me yourself."

"Find out what?"

"About your new villino! Don't think that I don't know. As soon as I go to my villino, for you I don't exist anymore and you go telling Elena before me."

"I didn't!" Melina said. Elena must have misinterpreted her yesterday at Mass.

"What didn't you do, tell her or buy a villino?"

Melina thought. This was her chance to set the facts straight, but the thought of her friends ringing each other from their holiday homes to find out more about this rumour…All that attention was irresistible. "I didn't tell Elena anything, but I can't confirm or deny whether I have bought a villino," she said importantly.

There was a moment's silence at the other end of the phone.

"I know what the problem is: you don't want to do a house-warming party. Leave it to me, Melina, I'll look after everything for you. Just give me a date and the address and you won't have to lift a finger."

"Oh, no, Peppina. I couldn't ask so much of you."

"Don't say that: this is what friends are for."

Melina suspected that Peppina would stop considering herself Melina's friend if she wasn't granted the privilege of organising the party. But what if Tanino couldn't get the house?

"If you won't name a date, I will. The fifteenth of August is a public holiday. Lunch at your new villino on August fifteenth," Peppina pressed on.

"I must ask Tanino first."

"Tut, tut. You don't ask your husband, you tell him. Unless you want to end up like Lucia, who must ask her husband's permission to breathe."

"But Tanino might have arranged something," Melina persisted.

"If he has arranged something and hasn't told you, all the worse for him."

***

Tanino didn't expect Melina to slip into bed with such a gloomy face. "Aren't you happy that I'm going to organise a holiday for us, dear?"

He had started to get excited at the idea. It would be nice to have some outside space, a little garden to tend, even if it wasn't his own. Giacomo had authorised him to help himself to anything that was ripe in exchange for tending the plants.

"I hope that your friend can give us the house, because my friends are coming for lunch on the fifteenth of August," she said sheepishly.

Goodness gracious! It had only been a couple of hours since he had aired the possibility of renting that house and Melina had already organised a lunch! "My dear, even after all these years you still manage to surprise me."

***

The Sicilian lemon and fennel sausages were sitting by the barbeque, the bread was cut and the pizza was in the oven.

Melina had made the sfincione pizza herself, kneading the dough, topping it with tomato sauce, onions, anchovies and grated caciocavallo cheese. She could never entertain in her home without cooking some of the food.

Even though, technically, this wasn't her home. Giacomo had let them the little cottage in the mountains for a peppercorn rent for two weeks, but her friends didn't need to know that.

The only person who could betray her secret was Tanino. A few minutes before the guests were due to arrive, Melina looked for him and found him in the garden.

"Dear, I need to tell you something."

He dropped the hosepipe, which swished left and right between the tomato plants like a crazed snake. "Don't tell me that the oven has burned the pizza."

"No, not that. Just, please don't look surprised if you hear that this is a housewarming party. My friends believe that we've bought this house."

He scrunched up his forehead. "Why would they…?"

"Melina, we're here!" Peppina chirped from the gate.

"Sorry, dear, I must go," Melina told Tanino and rushed to unlock the gate.

She saw car upon car filing up the dirt track to their gate. Peppina hadn't just invited a few close friends, but the entire parish.

If Melina had considered coming clean with her friends about the purchase of the villino, she definitely wasn't going to do that in front of all these people.

Aluminium trays of lasagne, pasta bakes, rice salads, couscous and cakes poured into her tiny cottage, spilled out of the back door and perched on rocks, tree branches and water butts.

All the while, Tanino's hosepipe continued to gush water onto the tomato patch, totally forgotten.

***

Tanino felt a little dizzy at the sheer number of cars snaking up the dirt track to their gate.

For a moment, he wondered if he should have asked permission from the local authorities to throw a party this big.

But he felt much better when he saw the trays of food pouring in and he sprang into action, welcoming guests, sorting out the parking and carrying bottles and dishes.

He was starting to enjoy playing host when he spotted someone emerging from one of the cars and his blood ran dry. It was Giacomo, the friend who had let them the cottage.

Why had he turned up? Had he been informed of the party and disapproved of it? Heaven forbid that he had heard from Melina's guests that the cottage was theirs! Tanino sprinted down the lane and locked his friend into a hug that was more like a tackle.

"My dear Giacomo, what a surprise!"

"The surprise is mine, too! My wife told me that we were going to a barbeque at a friend of a friend's. She couldn't tell me who nor where. So we followed the other cars and… ended up here!"

"I'm sorry, Giacomo, if I haven't invited you, but I hardly knew what was going on. My wife organised it all."

"It'll be a welcome change to be served in my home. The thought of watching you struggle with my barbeque makes me laugh already."

"Actually, old friend, I was thinking of sneaking out of the party. While the women chat, you could show me any interesting places to go near here."

Giacomo waggled a finger at him. "You just want to chicken out of lighting the barbeque. Don't worry, I'll help you. The secret is arranging the bricks in a certain way. Come, I'll show you."

***

"Ah, there you are! It's time to start the barbeque," Melina told Tanino when she saw him cross the gate with another man.

"Melina, this is Giacomo," Tanino said, moving his eyes strangely. He looked very pale.

"Good, you've found a friend. Please, get on with the barbeque," she said on her way to the kitchen. She had the feeling that Tanino wanted to tell her something, but she was too busy for chitchat now.

All through the meal she felt as if Tanino was trying to attract her attention, but so was everyone else. Whatever Tanino wanted to tell her, he could do it once everyone had gone. It wasn't every day that she hosted a party like this.

After the cakes, Peppina raised her voice. "May I have your attention, please?"

Everyone stopped talking and looked her way. "It's so wonderful that Melina and Tanino finally have their own little place in the country."

A man harrumphed and stood up. "I'm sorry to contradict you, but the house is mine."

Melina recognised the man that Tanino had just introduced to her and everything clicked.

People gasped. Melina felt like grabbing Tanino's hoe and digging a hole to hide somewhere near the centre of the earth.

"But if you want to buy this place, Tanino," the man added, turning to her husband, "I'd be happy to sell it to you. Every weekend I have to tend the plants, check the house, do repairs. I'm sick of it, but I haven't sold it because I felt that I should pass it on to my children like my parents passed it on to me. But I would be passing on to them a hot potato."

"I'd love to buy this house, Giacomo, but I can't afford it," Tanino admitted.

"I'll grant you the use of this place for as long as you live, in exchange for you looking after the house and the garden. Then you can enjoy it and my children can still inherit it."

"Giacomo, that would be wonderful!"

Tanino cried. "What do you say, Melina?"

Melina gave a little squeal which everyone must have taken as a yes, because they all clapped and whooped.

***

It was July and almost an entire year had passed since Giacomo had so kindly granted them perpetual use of his villino.

Tanino's enthusiasm for the place had grown with the tomatoes, the peppers and the aubergines that he had planted, but Melina had started to get stressed about the amount of preparation needed to move there for the summer.

As she stretched dustsheets over the sofa and the dining room table, she remembered Giovanna complaining to her, a year ago, about all the work she had to do every summer. And then there was dog care to arrange (thankfully, her sister-in-law didn't mind stepping in) and the fridge to empty.

She rallied together all the sauces, cheeses and hams that would not survive the hot car journey and went to knock on her neighbour's door.

"Hello, Giovanna. Would you like to use these things? We're going to the villino and I can't take them with me."

"Oh, yes, thank you. And I'll water your

plants for you!" Giovanna replied, excited.

"Thanks, but I need to find someone who will be here in August too."

"I will. Haven't I told you? I got fed up with all the work of keeping two houses functioning, so we've sold our villino. I'll happily look after your plants and your post. I can't believe that I can finally pay you back for all you've done for me, Melina." Giovanna smiled.

Melina thanked her and returned to her work in the flat. Mothballs needed to be put in cupboards, plug holes needed taping up and forwarding addresses needed to be given out.

But Melina didn't get much chance to carry on, because the doorbell rang over and over. As Giovanna spread the news that Melina was going on holiday, all the other people in the building flooded to her door, keen to pay her back for all the help she had given them every summer.

8. IT'S ALL RELATIVE

In his wife's family, blood was thicker than water, so Tanino wasn't surprised that Melina was catapulted into a high state of excitement when her sister, Cetta, asked them to host her grandson, Josh.

"Just think about it, Tanino. Having Josh here will be like having a small piece of Cetta with us!" Melina told him, misty-eyed.

The young man might well be a small piece of Cetta, but he was also a whole piece of himself, Tanino thought warily.

Cetta had left Sicily when she married a Scot, and had lived in Scotland ever since. Tanino and Melina weren't keen fliers, so they had never visited her. Cetta's grandson might well be their great-nephew, but they had never met him. As far as Tanino was concerned, he was a total stranger.

"How old is he?"

"He's just turned eighteen," Melina replied,

rushing around the flat with a measuring tape in hand.

So he wasn't just a stranger, but a young one, too, in the prime age for getting into trouble. Tanino was going to have to put down rules, curfews and limits to keep him on the straight and narrow, and he hated it. With only one daughter and one granddaughter, he had no experience of bringing up teenage boys.

What if the boy was a hooligan? A heavy drinker? He imagined himself scouring the taverns of Palermo, searching for the boy and dragging him home.

"What's he going to do while he's here?" Tanino asked gingerly.

"He's coming to improve his Italian, so I suppose he'll be studying Italian and sightseeing," Melina replied.

They would be expected to show the boy around the island. Tanino imagined having to fight his way through crowded tourist hotspots and sighed inwardly. "How long is he staying?"

"Only three months, unfortunately."

Three months? Didn't Cetta remember the Italian proverb which said that guests, like fish, go off after three days? Tanino felt a bead of sweat on his forehead. "I think it'll be long enough."

Melina stretched her measuring tape along

the bed of their spare room.

"Do you think that Josh will fit? I think that we should buy a new bed, just in case. And he'll also need a desk and a chair to study. And a lamp, of course," Melina added.

Now it wasn't just Tanino's forehead that was sweating, but his wallet, too.

"Why don't we just wait and see?" Tanino asked quietly, but Melina had already moved on to measuring the window.

"And new curtains!"

She was unstoppable.

That night, Tanino couldn't sleep. While Melina's sewing machine rattled away like a machine gun, he imagined the giant from "Jack and the Beanstalk" coming to live with them, sleeping on his new giant bed, and using curtains as table napkins.

But it was when Melina suggested they bought a TV for his room that Tanino really started to dislike their upcoming visitor.

"I think we've done enough. He can watch TV in the sitting room with us," Tanino declared.

"I suppose you will have to give him your chair. The view from the sofa isn't as good."

Tanino's chair was his sacred place and his throne.

"The view from the sofa will be just fine,"

he said curtly, and left the room before Melina made him resent their great-nephew even more.

***

Melina looked anxiously at the crowd pouring out of the arrivals gate. Still no sign of Josh.

If he didn't turn up very soon, Tanino would be furious. He had never enjoyed driving to the airport, but today he was being more than a little grumpy about it.

He had stubbornly refused to pay for parking, and was waiting outside in the car with an eye out for traffic wardens, just like a few months ago when her sister Cetta had come to visit. If she kept him waiting any longer, he would be furious by the time he met Josh.

In the last few days, Tanino had seemed almost unhappy about Josh's visit. But Josh was family—her own flesh and blood—so why would Tanino dislike him?

She scanned the arrivals again. Could Josh have already come out and she had missed him?

Even if Cetta hadn't sent her any recent photos of him, she would surely recognise her own family. Even if her eyes didn't tell her, her blood would! Someone tapped her on the shoulder and she turned.

A young man with ginger hair and freckles smiled at her. "Aunt Melina? I'm Josh," he said in Italian.

Melina stared at the stranger. The young man looked one hundred per cent Viking and zero per cent Sicilian. Where was the little piece of her sister?

"Hello," she said, smiling weakly. She offered him a hand to shake, but he enveloped her into a hug and kissed her on both cheeks.

"It's lovely to meet you at last, Auntie. Granny talks about you all the time," he said in perfect Italian.

"Thank you," she replied with all the enthusiasm she could muster.

Until a moment ago, she would have had no trouble matching Josh's enthusiasm and warmth, but right now she was struggling, and she felt bad about it. Surely looks didn't matter: family was family.

Tanino was waiting in the car just outside the exit, with a deep frown etched on his face.

"The traffic wardens have been twice and made trouble," he grumbled before even greeting Josh.

Melina was mortified. This wasn't the warm welcome she had planned for her sister's grandchild. "I'm sorry, Josh, if you're finding us a little tense. Tanino doesn't enjoy driving at the airport," she tried to explain.

"No problem at all. I wasn't even expecting to be picked up. I could have taken the bus. Thank you so much," Josh said good-naturedly.

He seemed a thoroughly nice young man.

***

Tanino was open-mouthed. The young man spoke perfect Italian and seemed perfectly nice. Josh was polite, kind and helpful. Nothing like the monster he had feared in his imagination.

While Melina's enthusiasm for her great-nephew seemed to have subsided a little, Tanino quickly turned into a great fan.

That same afternoon, he invited Josh to meet his friends at the café, and introduced him to the baker, the pizza maker and everyone who was anyone along their street.

Meanwhile, Melina kept herself busy in the kitchen.

The next day, Josh invited them both to go with him on a tour bus to the local attractions. Instead of driving through traffic and crowds, Tanino found himself following organised tours which Josh had arranged, enjoying the sights at leisure. He was having a blast and he couldn't imagine why he had been so worried and resentful about Josh's visit.

But he wasn't the only one enjoying Josh's

company. His granddaughter loved practising her English with Josh, his son-in-law enjoyed chatting with him about international politics, and his daughter, who was a teacher, liked to hear about the way schools worked in the UK. The only person Tanino didn't have to compete with for Josh's time was Melina.

***

Melina watched as her family gathered around the Sunday lunch table. Everyone vied for Josh's attention. He had charmed everyone because he was a delightful young man.

But Melina couldn't help mourning the piece of Cetta that he had failed to deliver to her.

It wasn't just the lack of physical resemblance. Many members of her family had a certain way of cocking their heads when they listened to someone, a way of clicking their tongue when they disliked something, or a characteristic laugh, which Cetta had inherited but Josh hadn't.

No matter how hard she tried, Melina couldn't find anything of Cetta in him. Josh seemed to have inherited absolutely nothing from her sister.

The phone rang. The others were engrossed in their conversations, so Melina got up to answer.

"Hello, Melina. It's Cetta," a familiar voice said at the other end of the phone.

A wave of nostalgia swept over Melina. "Hello, dear. Oh, how I miss you!"

"I miss you too, darling, and I miss my boy. How is he doing?"

"Everyone loves him. He's a delightful young man. So polite, kind, affectionate…"

"Thank you," Cetta said.

"… but he's not you."

"I know what you mean. Nobody can replace the person we're missing," Cetta said gravely. "Out of all the grandchildren, Josh is the one who looks the least like me. He's a copy of his other grandparents. But tell me, how do you find his Italian?"

"Excellent. It's been a big surprise. You never told me he could speak Italian so well," Melina replied, and she could almost hear her sister smile.

"I wanted it to be a surprise. You see, I taught him Italian. From the moment he was born, I talked to him in Italian, bought him books in Italian, showed him Italian DVDs. None of the other grandchildren were as interested as he was, so we carried on, even when he grew up. Every Friday he spends the night at my place and we call it 'Italian night'. He reads books to me, and I correct his pronunciation. You won't believe how many science fiction books we've read together!" she said, sounding pleased.

Melina felt her heart warm up. Josh might not have her sister's looks or mannerism, but in a way he was Cetta's handiwork, too. Her sister's patience, dedication and love had made Josh able to communicate with her in her own language. Whenever he spoke Italian to her, it was the fruit of Cetta's work and love.

She ended the call and returned to the dining room. "Auntie Melina, we were just waiting for you," Josh said as soon as she appeared in the door.

Melina smiled. Now that she knew how Josh had come to speak Italian so well, she felt as if a little piece of her sister was talking to her through him. Blood might be thicker than water, but love was thicker still.

9. IT'S THE THOUGHT THAT COUNTS

Tanino's birthday was coming up.

"What would you like for your birthday, dear?" Melina asked him, as she did every year.

"I don't need anything," he answered, like he did every year.

This time she was ready for it. "I've got my shoes on and my handbag on my arm. Unless you give me a suggestion now, it'll be a surprise."

"I hate surprises," Tanino grumbled. "Anyway, it makes no sense to buy me a present with my own money."

Those last three words stuck with Melina. Tanino hadn't meant to offend her, but he had said the truth and it stung. He was the breadwinner, and if she bought him a present, it would be with his own money. In their fifty years of marriage, every birthday gift she had ever given him had been bought with "his" money.

Deflated, Melina put down her bag, stepped out of her shoes and went to her bedroom, which was her favourite place to think or wallow. Could she resign herself to not buying her husband a present ever again? The answer was no.

So what could she do to give him a present that was all hers?

She picked up the phone, rang her sister-in-law and told her the problem.

"You could give him something that doesn't cost money, but time. You could cook him a special dish or give him a back massage," Fina suggested helpfully.

"I already do that from time to time, so it wouldn't be very special. If only I could get a job!"

There was silence at the other end of the phone and Melina could almost hear Fina smile.

"Actually, you could."

"Who's going to employ me when there are so many young people looking for work?"

"There are jobs that they don't know how to do," Fina replied.

With her primary school education, Melina couldn't imagine a single job where she was more qualified than somebody else, but Fina's words stoked her curiosity. "Tell me more."

"Come over and I'll show you."

Melina put on her shoes, grabbed her handbag and flew out of the house.

***

Fina's sitting room was covered in lengths of shiny white satin, rolls of lace, boxes of pearl and crystal beads. It could have been the set of a bridal show.

"Welcome to my workshop," Fina announced proudly. "The bridal shop downstairs gives me all the material and I sew the beads on to the fabric, following their designs."

Melina was speechless. She was sure that her eyes were glittering as much all those beads. Everything there was so beautiful! She would have sewn the beads on the lace without payment, just for the pleasure of working with those materials, but Fina was getting paid to do it! All over Palermo there would be happy brides wearing her work on their wedding day.

"The pay isn't huge and the work ebbs and flows," Fina admitted. "But it's good pocket money. I'm a little overwhelmed with work right now and I could do with some help," she added with a smile.

Melina grinned. "Count me in!"

***

Tanino woke up from his afternoon siesta to

an empty house again.

For the last week, he had hardly seen Melina. She was always out of the house.

What was she up to? He wasn't one of those men who demanded to know where their wives were at all times, but he was starting to get curious. That evening, at suppertime, he couldn't contain his curiosity any longer.

"Where have you been today?"

Melina stilled her fork and pursed her lips, as if she hadn't expected that question or wanted to answer it. This, of course, made Tanino more curious.

"Nowhere important," she replied vaguely.

"Why don't you want to tell me?"

"I've been at your brother's place, if you really want to know," she answered shiftily.

Instantly all of Tanino's alarm bells rang, because there could only be one reason for Melina being so cagey about visiting Ciccio and Fina just before his birthday. His knife and fork fell from his hands and onto the plate with a clatter.

"Please, don't! I hate birthday parties, and surprise ones are the worst!"

"I'm not organising any surprise party," she assured him, then changed the subject to the football on TV.

But Tanino was worried. He hadn't lived

with Melina for fifty odd years without learning to interpret every curve of her lips and expression of her face. His wife was hiding something.

After supper, he took the dog for his evening walk and called his brother from his mobile phone.

"Was Melina with you this afternoon?"

He hated sounding like a jealous husband, but he needed to know.

"Yes. She works with Fina every afternoon."

"Works?" He had to stop walking and lean against a wall to steady himself.

"Yes. Hasn't Melina told you?"

"No." His head spun a little. He wasn't sure what was more shocking: Melina getting a job or Melina not telling him.

Suddenly, he remembered saying to her that it made no sense for her to spend his money to buy him a birthday present. He had regretted his caddish comment as soon as he had said it, but it had clearly been too late. Melina's new job must have something to do with his insensitive words. He thanked his brother and closed the call.

He walked home in a daze. He had always been the breadwinner and Melina had always worked in the home. Were things going to change now?

***

For the first few days, sewing pretty beads on beautiful lace and chatting to her sister-in-law had been fun, but the novelty had now started to wear off.

The beads' holes were small and fiddly, the lace was dangerously delicate, and Melina's eyes and neck had started to ache. She and Fina had run out of things to chat about and had resorted to turning on the radio. Then there was the time pressure to deliver the work and get paid before Tanino's birthday.

That evening, Melina had stayed longer at Fina's and was home late for supper. Every muscle in her body ached and she wasn't looking forward to standing by the stove to cook supper.

To her pleasure and surprise, she found the table laid and a delicious-looking pizza waiting.

"When I saw that you were running late, I ordered some pizza," Tanino explained tentatively.

"That was a great idea! I'm so tired and achy."

"Sit down and I'll give you a neck and shoulder massage."

When was the last time Tanino had given her a massage?

"Yes, please."

After supper, when he offered to wash up and suggested she went to bed early, Melina became a little suspicious. Was he being so nice because he had done something wrong and was hoping to be forgiven? Was she going to discover something terrible in the morning?

But the next morning Tanino didn't reveal anything, so Melina forgot about it and went to her work.

***

When Melina wasn't home in time to cook supper the next evening again, Tanino went out and bought some roast chicken, chickpea fritters and potato croquettes. He resolved to ask her about her job that night, but when she got home looking even more exhausted than the day before, he didn't have the heart to trouble her.

How he regretted that careless comment! He wanted his wife back, rested and happy. Tomorrow, as soon as she woke up, he would tell her that they didn't need the extra money and that she could buy him all the presents she wanted.

***

Melina got up early and left the house before Tanino was up. Today was the final crunch: it was Tanino's birthday and she and Fina must deliver the goods to the shop and get paid if she was to buy Tanino's present.

They managed to complete the job before lunchtime, and with her hard-earned cash, Melina went straight to the model train shop. She knew just what Tanino would like.

***

Tanino was in a grump. On his birthday of all days, he had woken up to an empty bed and a scribbled message wishing him a happy birthday. Was he going to eat a takeaway meal on his own on his special day?

That evening, just when he was about to go down to the takeaway shop, Melina burst through the door, grinning like a madwoman.

"Happy Birthday!" she declared. "I got you a present, but this time I bought it with money I earned."

She handed him a large box. The wrapping paper was printed with pictures of trains.

"Oh, darling, you didn't have to do that! I'm so sorry about what I said," Tanino told his wife.

"Don't worry. Work has been fun."

Those words worried him even more.

"Does this mean that you will carry on working?"

"Only if Fina needs help," Melina replied. "The work was fun, but it was terribly tiring on the eyes and the neck. I'm much happier with my job here."

Tanino felt a weight lift off his shoulders.

"So you won't be away from home for hours and hours every day anymore?"

"No."

That was the best present by far!

Melina took off her coat and rushed to the kitchen, where she was about to put her apron on, but Tanino stopped her.

"How about we celebrate with dinner at that new little restaurant they've just opened down the road?" he suggested. "But first, you need a shoulder massage."

***

Since she had given him that model train set on his birthday, Melina hardly saw Tanino anymore.

His brother had given him exclusive use of his spare room to build it, so Tanino was always at his brother's flat.

Fina reported that the two men were having a lot of fun with the model, which was coming along very nicely.

It was lovely to hear, but tonight supper had been ready for some time and was growing cold.

Finally, the door opened and Tanino walked in.

"I'm sorry I'm late."

He sounded terribly tired and he looked stiff.

"Are you alright?"

"Yes. I just have a little ache in my shoulders from all that fiddly work. I don't suppose you could give me a neck and shoulder massage?"

10. SINK OR SWIM

Melina drained the cooking pot into the sink, but the water didn't immediately flow away.

"This sink is still blocked. When will you fix it?" she snapped at Tanino, fishing the colander out of the flood.

She had asked her husband to deal with the blocked sink a few times already, but he still hadn't done it.

"I'll do it after lunch," Tanino reassured her.

But after lunch was her husband's siesta time, Melina thought, and when he woke up he would no doubt have urgent errands to do. Then it was supper time, and after that it was dark. He never worked in the dark.

Melina didn't think about it again until the next morning, when she was back from Palermo's Capo Market.

She was rinsing some cooked beetroot when the water pooled in the sink again. It was purple-red, like she imagined the blood in her veins.

Melina vented her frustration with her next-door neighbour, Giovanna, who was out on her balcony putting her laundry out to dry.

"Tell Tanino that if he doesn't deal with it right now, you will fix it yourself," Giovanna suggested.

"But I don't know how to fix it," Melina replied.

"That's the whole point. He knows that, and he dreads you trying, so he'll immediately do the job for you."

It sounded like a great idea.

***

Tanino had fallen asleep in front of a Western and was dreaming of cowboys, mustangs and bison. He was just about to lasso a runaway bison when a voice intruded into his dream. "If you don't fix the sink right now, I'll do it myself!"

It must have been the bison trying to distract him, but it was a silly thing to tell a cowboy. If there really was a sinkhole, what could he do about it? Guns, spurs and ropes were no good to deal with a sinkhole.

He grunted and continued to pursue the cheeky animal.

***

What was it about Western movies that her husband liked so much? Actors who looked like they hadn't had a bath in years moved over landscapes even more parched than Sicily!

Still, Tanino was so mesmerised by them that it was always impossible to get more than a monosyllable out of him when he was watching one.

"Are you going to fix it or am I?" Melina asked him again, just to be sure.

No sound.

"Then I'm going to do it, Tanino!"

He grunted again. This time she couldn't doubt that it was a yes. Her plan had backfired. Now she had to fix the sink herself.

She rushed to Giovanna and told her what had happened.

"What am I going to do now? I have no idea how to unblock a sink."

"Then you'll have to learn."

Melina's heart sank. She and Tanino had always had very clear roles. She had always done the domestic chores, while he worked outside the home and did house repairs.

"I'm not even sure that I can use the plunger properly," she admitted.

"It doesn't matter. You're a clever woman and you can learn. I will help you."

***

First they tried the plunger, but the sink was still blocked.

"We must turn off the water at the stopcock," Giovanna declared.

"What's that?" Melina asked, confused.

"It's a switch that turns the water off from the whole flat."

Luckily, Giovanna's flat was a mirror image of Melina's, so she knew exactly where to find everything and led Melina onto the balcony. There was the shiny red tap.

Melina had seen it many times, but had never paid it any attention. She turned off the stopcock and went back into the kitchen.

"We have to unscrew the U-bend. That's where things usually get stuck."

Melina opened the cabinet under the sink and saw the pipes in the shape of a letter "U". How did her friend know so much?

"We need a bowl to put under it because water will come out."

Melina got the washing-up bowl and made space for it among the cleaning products.

They had just started unscrewing the nuts of the U-bend when Giovanna's mobile phone rang.

"Sorry, Melina, I have to go. You know what to do, don't you?"

"I'll be just fine," Melina lied, forcing a

smile.

She would have to face the mysteries lurking under her sink on her own.

As soon as the U-bend came off, lots of water splashed into the bowl. There were tomato seeds, grit, soil, and her lost earring! This was starting to be fun.

Melina poked into the U-bend and recovered more lost items, including her grandchild's hairclip. No wonder the sink was blocked!

She screwed the U-bend back in place, turned the stopcock on and opened the kitchen tap.

Oh, no. The problem must be somewhere else along the pipes. She unscrewed the U-bend again, but this time she carried on, taking apart the other sections of piping all the way to the wall.

Finally, on the last bit, she found a plug of fat. She scooped it out with great satisfaction, feeling like a truly accomplished woman, the queen of the waterways.

When it was time to put everything back together, she realised that she had made a terrible mistake.

Instead of placing the pipes on the floor in the order in which she'd taken them apart, she had scattered them randomly and hadn't the faintest idea how they went back together. Who could she ask for help?

Giovanna was out and she could hardly ask Tanino! By agreeing to her fixing the sink, he had set her a challenge. Calling a plumber was out of the question: it would mean admitting defeat.

Suddenly, she had a better idea. She shoved all the pipes into the cabinet, closed it and left.

***

Tanino the cowboy had rounded up all the recalcitrant bison, tamed the proud mustangs and woken up feeling rejuvenated.

He went to the toilet, then to wash his hands. No water came out of the tap.

Hadn't Melina asked him to fix one of the sinks? He had thought that it was just a small drainage issue, but this looked more serious.

"Melina?"

No answer. She must be out. He tried the other taps, but there was no water anywhere in the house. Did the problem affect just his flat, or the whole building?

He rushed downstairs to the porter who guarded the entrance and looked after the building.

"I haven't turned the water off, and nobody has reported any problems. Is the stopcock turned on?" the porter asked him.

"Of course!" Tanino replied. No one would have touched it other than him, and he would remember if he had turned it off.

When he got back to his flat and checked, just in case, he found the tap in the off position! How could it be? He didn't remember doing it.

Maybe one of the pigeons, which were getting bolder and bolder by the day, had sat on it. He turned the water back on and tried the kitchen tap. The water gushed out of the tap beautifully.

Oh, no! Water was leaking out of the bottom of the cabinet! He yanked the doors open. Inside the cabinet was a scene of devastation. This wasn't any ordinary leak. The sink's pipes were scattered among the detergent bottles as if there had been an explosion.

He should have listened to his wife and fixed the problem while it was still fixable! Now that the pipes had burst, he had no choice but to call the plumber.

He mopped the water, closed the cabinet and set off briskly to the plumber's workshop just down the road.

***

Melina returned to her flat with her confidence restored. She had knocked on the door of her neighbour upstairs and had made a sketch of the way the pipes were connected under her kitchen sink. Now there was no reason why she shouldn't be able to put her sink back together.

She connected each section of piping with the enthusiasm of a child playing with Lego. What fun!

Soon the sink was back together and draining beautifully. She had done it! From now on, she would never think that a job was beyond her until she had at least tried it.

She cleaned the earring she had recovered from the U-bend and put it on with its companion. Now she was ready for Tanino to come home and be amazed at her work.

***

"I've never heard of exploding drains. I'm very curious," the plumber admitted, following Tanino back to the building.

As soon as they walked into the flat, Melina greeted Tanino from the kitchen. "Hello, darling!"

Tanino was puzzled and a little wary. How could she be so cheerful? Wasn't she mad at him for letting their plumbing problems get out of control?

"We have a visitor, Melina," he told her, trudging slowly down the corridor behind the plumber. He dreaded having to admit to Melina that he had had to call professional help.

"Where's the broken sink?" the man asked.

"There's no broken sink. I've repaired it." She smiled smugly.

The man's smile didn't conceal his disbelief.

"Alright. Where's the sink that was broken?"

She opened the cabinet. Every pipe was in its proper place.

"Have you tried turning the tap on?" Tanino asked her, imagining another explosion as soon as she did.

"Of course."

She turned the tap on, and the water drained beautifully down the sink and through the pipes. Incredible!

The plumber checked every seal. "It's all fine, Signor Tanino. Whatever it was, your good lady has fixed it."

Melina beamed as if she had just been given a medal.

As soon as the plumber had left, Tanino turned to his wife.

"You have never touched a sink before. How did you do it?"

She smiled. "I picked it up as I went along. Now, is there anything else you need my help with?"

11. WORK IT OUT

Tanino suspected he was about to say something unwise, but he said it anyway.

"Isn't that skirt a bit tight, Melina? It looks like you're about to burst out of it."

The hobs flared orange as the salt that Melina was sprinkling on the grill pan fell on the flames.

"Are you saying I'm fat?"

"No. Only that the skirt is too tight," he reasoned, immediately regretting his comment.

She stabbed a knife through the heart of a cauliflower.

Tanino wished he could take back his words. "I just mean that you should buy a new skirt."

"So I dress shabbily?"

She poured salt into the bubbling pot, which foamed furiously.

Tanino scuttled out of the kitchen to the safety of the sitting room and turned on the TV.

***

Tanino forgot all about the incident until the next day at lunchtime, when he noticed that Melina had cooked only enough pasta for one.

She dished it out onto a plate and put it down before him. She was having salad.

Fearful of saying the wrong thing, Tanino ate in silence, all the time feeling Melina's eyes on his plate and hearing the salad leaves crunching between her teeth.

Eventually, he couldn't take it any longer.

"This plate is too much for me," he lied. "Would you like some?"

Her face lit up.

"It would be a shame to throw it in the bin," she said, sweeping the contents of Tanino's plate onto hers and tucking in.

But at five o'clock Tanino was ravenous, so he sneaked down to the café, bought an arancina rice ball and strolled to the park to eat it in peace.

***

When Tanino opened the door to his flat that evening, no smell of cooking filled his nostrils. He braced himself for the worst.

Two plates of salad sat mockingly on the table. The leaves didn't even have the sheen of an oily dressing.

A sweeping glance round the kitchen

confirmed that the two salads were not a side dish. There wasn't even bread to go with them. Tanino groaned.

"Melina, we can't have just salad for supper."

"The health experts say that people should eat light at suppertime," she replied loftily.

Tanino knew this had nothing to do with health experts and everything to do with his comment about the skirt. Melina must have decided that, if she kept him on the same diet, she would find it easier to stick to it.

"The best way to lose weight is exercise. Starving is not the way to go."

"Nobody is starving," she retorted. "Look how much salad there is!"

All the same, she got up and pulled a tin of tuna out of the cupboard.

***

The tuna wasn't enough. At midnight, Tanino was awake with a grumbling stomach.

When Melina was sleeping, he slipped out of bed, padded to the kitchen and opened the fridge. To his disappointment, all he found was lettuce and raw broccoli.

He opened the freezer. Alas, the tub of ice cream had gone. In its place were frozen mountains of peas, broad beans and vegetable soup.

If he used the microwave, or rummaged for a pot and used the hobs, he would wake Melina. So he pulled out a packet of frozen peas and popped them into his mouth one by one.

***

As she lay awake in bed with an empty tummy, Melina pondered Tanino's words: "The best way to lose weight is exercise."

She was still awake when Tanino shuffled out of bed and plodded to the kitchen. Poor Tanino, he was hungry too!

The next morning, as soon as Tanino had left the house, Melina found a tracksuit and put it on.

The way the elasticated trousers bulged over her tummy confirmed her resolve to visit the gym. Exceptionally, she left before finishing the domestic chores.

Her first stop was the shoe shop, where she asked for a pair of trainers.

"What do you need them for?" the assistant asked.

"Losing weight."

The girl looked confused. "Aerobics? Zumba?"

"Whatever you suggest."

The girl returned with three pairs of trainers. Her choice was black, grey or candyfloss pink.

"I'll take the pink ones," Melina said, reaching for the box.

The entrance to the gym was a long corridor sloping down to the basement of a block of flats. Pictures of muscly men and women eyed Melina from the walls and she felt uneasy.

"How can I help?" the receptionist asked.

"My friends told me that you do ladies' classes."

"We do," the girl replied. "We have a few places left on the Thursday class."

"But I need it today!" Melina exclaimed.

"I'm sorry, but there are no classes today. You need an assessment first, too."

"What for?"

"Our instructor, Giulia, needs to know where you want to be, then work out a personalised fitness plan. Here she is! Giulia, I have a new client for you."

A woman with glossy hair pulled into a tight ponytail sauntered towards them.

"This lady is keen to start as soon as possible," the receptionist told her.

"Great," Giulia replied. "Follow me."

They entered a room packed full of machines. Running machines groaned and squeaked under the feet of people rushing like hamsters on their wheels. Complicated systems of pulleys, chains and counterweights were operated by men glistening with sweat. When the metal weights reached the bottom, they clanged like shackles and chains, startling Melina.

Giulia tapped away on a tablet, asking Melina her details and her goals. Then she led her to a room with scales, callipers and tape measures.

Having been weighed and measured, Melina was led into a room clad in mirrors. She discovered that pink dumbbells were not as light and fluffy as they looked, and that she owned muscles that she didn't know how to operate.

Movements that she didn't realise the human body could do magically came to her, which she found exhilarating.

Until Giulia led her to a room full of elastic bands and rubber balls. There the real work started.

***

Tanino had taken precautions against a zero-calorie lunch. He had filled his tummy with fried calzone at the café earlier.

"I'm home!" he declared, stepping through the door.

No reply.

He peered into the kitchen. Nothing was bubbling on the hobs, there was no salad on the table and no trace of Melina.

He already deeply regretted his comment about the skirt! How much longer must he be punished?

Then a groan came from the sitting room. He found Melina sprawled on the sofa with her eyes closed.

"What happened?" Tanino exclaimed.

Melina opened one eye and closed it again. "I can't move. I can't bend my legs. And my feet are killing me."

A pair of pink trainers lay on the floor as if they had been hastily pulled off.

Only then did Tanino notice that Melina was wearing a tracksuit.

"What have you been up to?"

"I've joined the gym."

So she hadn't had an accident! "You must have been able to bend your legs to walk home," he observed.

Melina darted him a sideways glance before closing her eyes again. "They seized after I got home."

"You should go to bed."

"There's no way I can get up. I might have to sleep right here tonight."

Tanino worried about his lunch. He'd learnt to cook once, when Melina had pretended to be sick, but he was out of practice.

"Also," Melina continued, "there's laundry in the washing machine and I didn't get a chance to sweep the floor before I went out. Or tidy the bedroom."

"Don't worry, I'll do it. But what about lunch?"

She rolled a hand dramatically in the air, without opening her eyes. "Food is the last thing on my mind."

Food was never the last thing on Tanino's mind. "Okay. I'll get some pizza from the baker's. Would you like anything?"

"No, thanks." She sighed and crossed her arms on her chest.

He had told her to exercise more. It was entirely his fault that she was in that state now.

He left the flat feeling very guilty, so when he got to the baker's, instead of pizza, he bought a small bread bun of the kind he didn't like.

***

"Melina, are you all right? We missed you in church tonight," Anna said on the telephone.

Melina was supposed to help with the flower arrangements.

"I'm sorry. I went to the gym this morning and now I'm like a block of wood. Like Pinocchio before Geppetto gave him hinges."

"Whatever gave you the idea of going to the

gym?" Anna was incredulous.

"Tanino made a comment about my skirt being tight."

"Oh, I hate it when men do that! How dare they tell us how we should look?"

"As we're stuck with each other for better and worse, maybe it's kind to make things a little easier, more comfortable. Or they might look for comfort elsewhere."

"Not at seventy-three!"

"Charlie Chaplin was seventy-three when he fathered his last child."

Silence fell. Anna's husband was seventy-two.

"Where is this gym?" Anna asked timidly.

***

The next day, Melina went to the gym with Anna. It was Thursday so the ladies' class was on. There was music and, even if she didn't always manage to follow the steps, Melina had a blast.

When she got home, Tanino was waiting expectantly for her. "How was your gym?"

For a moment, Melina wondered whether to tell Tanino the truth, but she hadn't quite forgiven him for the skirt comment. "Blood, sweat and tears."

Tanino's face crumpled.

"Oh, Melina, I can't bear to see you suffer! I

should have never made that silly comment! You are perfect! Please, come back to me, my darling!"

"Well, if you insist," she replied coyly.

He steered her to the kitchen, where the table was laid with every bounty from the bakery, café and greengrocer's.

Melina felt her heart warm like the hot custard inside a cornetto croissant.

"Isn't it a little too much for two people?"

"Eat what you like and leave the rest. Eat to your heart's content." Tanino squeezed her.

The doorbell rang and they jumped. It was Rosanna, their daughter.

"I have a job interview tomorrow and I wondered if Mum has finished the hem on my skirt."

"What skirt?" Tanino asked.

"My skirt I gave her a while ago to sew the hem with her machine."

Melina slapped her forehead.

"I had forgotten! I found the skirt in my cupboard and, not giving it another thought, wore it!"

Melina and Tanino looked at each other and burst into laughter.

"What's this?" Rosanna asked, confused.

When they finished laughing, they told her all that had happened and invited her to lunch, as there was plenty for three.

12. ONE HUMBLE REQUEST

Melina had woken up in a miserable mood. It was one of those wet, gloomy days and she had a stiff neck.

"My neck hurts," she told her husband as they sat at the breakfast table.

"You need a massage," Tanino said, getting up from his chair and abandoning his coffee.

He laid his warm hands on her shoulders and Melina felt instantly better.

But instead of caressing her gently, as Melina had hoped, he started kneading her shoulders as if they were bread dough. He pressed his thumbs into every knot of her sore muscles as if he were burying rosemary into a focaccia bread.

"Ouch! Enough, please," she protested.

"I know it hurts, but it's good for you," he replied without stopping.

By the time he had finished, Melina had tears in her eyes and wondered if her neck had grown longer. She had to admit that it felt a lot better. Unfortunately, though, her mood hadn't improved.

"Thank you," she said feebly.

"You mustn't carry weights with your sore neck. I'll do the grocery shopping today," Tanino offered.

No, this couldn't be: grocery shopping was when she met friends in the streets, chatted with the shopkeepers and got cooking inspiration from the food that was on offer.

"I'll be fine."

"Pulling the trolley is likely to make your neck worse. Why risk it if you've got me?" Tanino asked.

He got the shopping trolley out of the storeroom. He clearly wasn't going to give up.

Melina watched him from the window as he pulled the trolley down the street and disappeared round the corner.

She felt a little lonely. It was very kind of Tanino to give her a massage and do the shopping. He was certainly doing all the right things, so why was she so unhappy?

***

Provide, protect and prosper: these were what Tanino had signed up for, more than fifty years ago, when he and Melina had married. They all still applied, and he would continue to do his best at them.

He filled the trolley with enough fruit and vegetables for two days, in case Melina still wasn't up to shopping tomorrow, and asked the baker to deliver their bread to their flat for the rest of the week.

Then he bought enough fish and chicken to fill the freezer so that Melina wouldn't have to go to the fishmonger or the butcher for weeks. When his trolley was full, he turned around and headed home. Melina was going to be delighted.

But she wasn't. When he got home, he found her gloomier than when he had left. Not even the faintest smile formed on her lips as he showed her the sea bream, the hake, the cockles and mussels. When he pulled the chicken goujons out of the trolley, she looked positively alarmed.

"There's enough to eat for months!" she exclaimed.

"Yes, so you won't have to go to the fishmonger or the butcher for a while."

He grinned, but she still didn't smile.

"There won't be enough space in the freezer," she moaned.

"We'll make space," he said.

They both turned to go to the fridge freezer and bumped into each other.

"Ouch!" Melina cried out.

Had he hurt her?

"Sorry, dear. Is it your neck?"

She pursed her lips as if she was sucking on a lemon. "I've hit my little toe against the chair's leg." She pointed to the broken chair—the one he had been meaning to fix for ages but never got round to—with its leg sticking out at an odd angle, waiting to trip someone.

"I'll repair it right now."

But first he accompanied his hobbling wife to another chair, got some ice and put it on her toe.

"I'll get chilblains," she protested.

"You don't want your toe to swell."

Melina accepted the ice pack with the enthusiasm of a child taking medicine.

Tanino left her with the ice and got his toolbox out of the storeroom.

He was almost done repairing the chair when Melina called from the other room.

"The ice has melted!"

"You don't need it anymore," he called back from the kitchen.

"But it's making the floor wet."

"Then don't get up until I've mopped it."

Heaven forbid she slipped and hurt some other part of her body!

By the time Tanino had finished repairing

the chair and mopping the floor, it was already lunchtime, and he was very hungry. Thank goodness he had bought some ready-made pizza from the baker so that Melina wouldn't have to cook. He popped it into the oven, and when it was nicely warmed, he called Melina to the table.

She didn't eat more than a morsel.

"I thought you liked our baker's pizza," he said.

"I'm not very hungry."

"Is your neck hurting?"

She nodded, pushing the slice of pizza around her plate.

"You should put a hot pack on it."

"I don't want it."

"You've got rheumatism because our flat is too damp. You need heat."

Tanino abandoned his pizza and went to the central heating control panel to change the timer.

He took a bite of his pizza, which was now lukewarm and rubbery. He was starting to feel disheartened. Melina's gloominess must be rubbing off on him. No matter how hard he tried, he seemed unable to make things better for her. And every time he tried and failed, he felt inadequate, powerless and a little guilty.

If he couldn't ban cold, damp days from

Sicily, maybe he should have looked for a job in the tropics and moved his family there when he was much younger. Or he could have got himself a better-paid job, bought a second home in the Canary Islands, and retired there with Melina. He sighed and turned on the TV.

It was the one o'clock news. Images of a flood reeled on the screen. Melina turned to him. Would she ask him to "fix" the floods too, he thought in a moment of panic.

"Could you pass me the bread?" she asked him instead.

***

Melina could see that Tanino was trying his best to help her, so why was she still feeling so miserable? Her neck wasn't hurting very much anymore, and her toe was long forgotten.

All the same, she felt more miserable now than when she had got up in the morning.

Tanino had washed up after lunch and was sitting on his favourite armchair in front of the TV, with their dog on his lap. She wished there was space for her on the chair too, but there wasn't, so she sat on the sofa.

"Why don't you join me here?" she asked him from the sofa.

"I'm fine here," he replied, stroking Bello.

She felt a little left out, so she stretched out her hand towards the armchair, hoping that

Tanino would reach out and hold it.

He didn't notice.

"Tanino?"

He heaved a sigh and turned to her.

"What now?"

She felt her heart whither like a leaf in winter.

"I was only going to ask you—"

"What else do you want me to fix for you?" he interrupted her in an exasperated tone.

"I don't want you to fix anything," she replied with a knot in her throat.

"I've tried all morning to fix your problems, but this is as far as I can go!" Tanino replied.

Had she asked him all that? She thought hard, but couldn't remember doing it.

"I didn't ask you any of this," she said, surprised.

"What about your sore neck? Didn't you want me to fix it?"

"No. If I had wanted my neck fixed, I'd have gone to the physio. I only told you about it because…"

Why had she?

"…I guess I was looking for sympathy, a kind word, maybe"— she hesitated—"a cuddle."

"When you hurt your toe, you weren't accusing me of not having fixed the chair?"

"No, and my toe wasn't hurting very much. Certainly not enough for ice."

"And all you wanted was a hug?" Tanino asked.

"Yes, and some words of commiseration."

"And I failed completely," he said.

"But it's never too late," Melina pointed out.

"I see."

Tanino smiled and got up from his chair. He sat on the sofa, put an arm around her and pulled her to himself.

Tension drained out of her muscles, her neck didn't feel too stiff anymore, and she leaned her head on his shoulder.

"How am I doing now?" Tanino asked.

"Much better." Melina smiled.

The End

Other books by Stefania Hartley

Collections of short stories:

Keeping It Cool
Sand, Sea and Tamburello
To Be Loved
Welcome to Quayside
A Season of Goodwill
Tales from the Parish
What's Yours is Mine
Stars Are Silver
A Slip of the Tongue
Confetti and Lemon Blossom
Fresh from the Sea

Romance novellas:

The Italian Fake Date
Sweet Competition for Camillo's Café
Second Chances at Mamma's Trattoria
Under Far Eastern Skies

Cosy mysteries:

Father Roberto and the Missing Money

ABOUT THE AUTHOR

Stefania was born in Sicily and immediately started growing, but not very much. She left her sunny island after falling head over heels in love with an Englishman, and now she lives in the UK with her husband and their three children.

Having finally learnt English, she's enjoying it so much that she now writes novels and short stories which have been longlisted, shortlisted, commended, and won prizes.

If you have enjoyed these stories, please consider leaving a review.

If you want to hear when she's releasing a new book, sign up for her newsletter: www.stefaniahartley.com/subscribe

You'll also receive an exclusive short story.

Printed in Great Britain
by Amazon

58114791R00078